THE YOUNG PERRY MASON

BURNETT LEE DORRIS

First Edition

NEWMAN SPRINGS PUBLISHING
320 Broad Street
Red Bank, NJ 07701

First originally published by Newman Springs Publishing 2023

ISBN 979-8-89061-480-3 (Paperback)
ISBN 979-8-89061-481-0 (Digital)

Printed in the United States of America

The Case of the Serial Killer
A drama fiction story
And
Dennis Edwards and the Temptations
A nonfiction story

The Case of the Serial Killer

This story is dedicated to—

Raymond Burr (May 21, 1917, to September 12, 1993) as Perry Mason
William Hopper as Paul Drake
Barbara Hale as Ms. Della Street (Perry Mason's secretary)

—who are no longer with us and whom we will always love and remember.

Preface

Raymond Burr will always be, to me, the greatest of all time.

From his roles as the villain in many movies to portraying a lawyer in the film *A Place in the Sun* and the iconic lawyer Perry Mason.

He also played Ironside. To me, Raymond Burr will always be the best actor, along with William Hopper and Barbara Hale.

The Son of Perry Mason is a fictional story about a young man named Burt Mason, the son of Perry Mason, who becomes a lawyer like his father.

Like father, like son, Burt always finds a way to win a case, no matter what it is.

In this story, a man is accused of being a serial killer, and Burt Mason has to find the real killer and free an innocent man before he is executed.

But will Burt catch the killer in time?

From the Beginning

The date was May 14, 1990, in San Diego, California.

A young man named Burt Mason, along with his father, Perry Mason, attended his son's graduation from San Diego University, where he became a lawyer.

Burt, just like his father, Perry, had studied law for ten years to become the best lawyer, following in his father's footsteps.

Mr. Perry Mason was present, along with Paul Drake and Perry Mason's secretary, Ms. Della Street.

They were all celebrating Burt's graduation at the university and at Burt's home in San Diego.

Many other people who knew Burt were also in attendance. Burt was engaged to a woman named Audrey Taylor.

They planned to get married once Burt started making a lot of money as a lawyer, just like his father, Perry Mason.

Their plan was to move to Los Angeles to be with Perry.

Burt was thirty-two years old, and Perry now seventy-three years old.

Burt attended law school at San Diego, California University when he was twenty-three and completed his studies at the age of thirty-two. He obtained his law degree and became a licensed lawyer. Burt took on his first major case while Perry Mason had just finished defending a young woman named Mrs. Joan Rivers in a murder case. She was wrongly accused, and Perry won the case, setting her free. Mrs. Rivers returned home as an innocent woman.

Perry Mason worked on numerous cases, many of which involved murder. Perry was exceptionally skilled in his profession, with the assistance of Della and Paul.

Mason would often tell his son Burt that maybe one day Della and Paul would assist him as well.

Burt merely laughed at Perry's comment. A few months after Burt's graduation, he and his fiancée packed their belongings and moved to Los Angeles, where Perry resided.

Perry Mason Becomes Ill

Perry and Burt collaborated on numerous murder cases and other legal matters. Burt expressed his desire for his own office, and he eventually obtained one while still working closely with Perry for a few more years.

Around 1991, Perry Mason fell ill and visited a doctor accompanied by his wife, Isabella Ward. During the examination, x-rays revealed tumors on Perry's kidneys, which deeply saddened Burt, as well as their friends and family.

Perry Mason's health deteriorated, and unfortunately, the doctors could not offer any effective treatments for Perry's condition.

Realizing the severity of his illness, Perry informed Burt that he would retire, prompted by the doctor's revelation that the cancer had spread to his liver.

Perry shared with Burt that he was dying and expressed his desire to spend his remaining time on his Sonoma County ranch near Healdsburg.

The Ending of Perry Mason When He Dies and His Legacy

Burt continued working in Los Angeles, and he would always go and visit Perry whenever he had the time. But on September 12, 1993, Burt received a phone call from Isabella that Perry, her husband, had passed away.

Oh, how it hurt Burt, and despite being in the middle of a case, he had to give it to another lawyer and take a plane to Sonoma, where Perry was. Paul Drake and Della Street went with Burt and his wife Audrey.

It was a very sad day that day. Perry had written a letter to Burt just before he passed away. It said:

> Dear Burt,
>
> I am so very proud of you because you have become a lawyer. I am not expecting you to be like me, but I know you are going to be the best lawyer that you can be. And I also know Paul and Della are going to help you throughout your career as being the best lawyer that you can be. And I know you are not going to let me down, my son. You may not win all the cases, but just do the best you can. I will always love you, and I

am going to miss you. And please remember me
as I was. Love you, son, and goodbye.

Perry

Burt couldn't help but cry because of Perry's passing and the way he died. Isabella, Burt's mother, was also in tears.

It was a whole month before they would have Perry's memorial service, which got started on October 1, 1993. Burt approached his mother and asked, "Mother, what are you going to do now that Dad is gone? What are you going to do about the ranch? You cannot live here all by yourself. Why don't you put it up for sale and move to Los Angeles with us?"

Isabella replied, "No, no, I can't live there. Perry and I love it here. I never did like big cities like Los Angeles, my son. I am going to stay. You go ahead, Burt. You have a family you've got to take care of. I am going to stay here."

"Well, Mother, okay," Burt accepted her decision.

They held Perry's burial at the Fraser Cemetery in New Westminster, British Columbia. The memorial service took place at the Pasadena Playhouse, with only close family and friends in attendance.

Burt was feeling lost and cold at first. It was like his whole life had died along with Perry. But after Isabella talked to Burt, he got himself together because he had a wife to take care of. Paul and Della expressed their condolences before heading back to Los Angeles.

"Mother, I will be keeping in touch with you from time to time," Burt assured her.

Della took Isabella by her hand and said, "I am so sorry about Perry, Mrs. Mason."

Isabella replied, "Thank you, Paul."

Paul said, "You take care, Mrs. Mason."

Isabella thanked him. Paul kissed Isabella on her jaw and said again, "You take care, Mrs. Mason."

"Goodbye, Mother," said Burt.

The Killings

They all boarded the plane to Los Angeles. When he returned, Burt found lots and lots of pictures of Perry almost everywhere, even with Isabella as a child. Burt, Paul, and Della went home for the weekend.

In the months leading up to Perry's death, there had been a series of killings of women from Bakersfield all the way through San Francisco, Santa Rosa, and San Jose counties. There was a serial killer on the loose, and the killings continued in Los Angeles County. The police and the FBI were on the case, finding various pieces of evidence. However, the identity of the killer remained unknown.

Burt would see the news and read about it in the newspapers, worrying about Isabella living alone with all these killings happening. The serial killer wore a mask, making it difficult for some of the women who managed to escape to identify him. Whenever a woman saw a masked man, they would think he was the killer and call the police. But upon pointing out the man to the police, they would realize it was the wrong person.

The killer used a blue rope to tie the women's arms and legs, and then he would pull out a knife from his pocket and stab them.

A Woman Had Just Got Murdered by a Serial Killer

It was November 9, 1993, Saturday, at 9:30 p.m.

A man named Chris Holden was at home watching television, minding his own business, when he decided to go to a store near his home in downtown Los Angeles at nine-thirty that night. Unbeknownst to him, the killer had spotted a beautiful woman walking down the street and hurried into an alley to intercept her. The killer had donned a mask and positioned himself at the end of the alley, waiting for the woman to pass by.

Coincidentally, Chris Holden was also walking down the same street wearing a similar mask. As the woman crossed the alley, the killer grabbed her by the face and forcefully pulled her into the alley. She began screaming for her life as he subjected her to a brutal beating. Despite her resistance, the killer managed to overpower her, tearing off her clothes and assaulting her.

In the midst of the assault, the woman managed to bite the killer's hand, causing him to release his grip and allowing her to scream for help. It was at this moment that Chris, who had been walking down the street, heard the woman's cries and rushed towards the source of the screams, leading him to the alley. Meanwhile, the killer retrieved his knife and began stabbing the woman multiple times, resulting in blood splattering across the alley.

Chris glanced down the alley and witnessed the horrific scene of the killer repeatedly stabbing the woman. Determined to intervene, Chris pursued the killer, who, upon seeing Chris approaching, hastily pulled up his pants and fled the scene, leaving behind his bloodied knife and gloves. Simultaneously, several people in the vicinity heard the screams and promptly dialed 911 to alert the police.

Police Officer J. T. Tippit and his partner, who were patrolling nearby, received the call from the police station and swiftly drove toward the alley with sirens blaring and lights flashing.

A Innocent Man Has Just Been Accused of Murder

As the police were on their way, Chris came running down the alley with his mask on and saw the woman. He tried to help her, but it was too late—she was already dead.

Police officer Tippit spotted Chris and drove down the alley in pursuit, with other officers blocking Chris from escaping. They approached him with guns in hand.

Officer Tippit and his partner shouted, "HOLD IT RIGHT THERE AND DON'T YOU MOVE AND PUT YOUR HANDS UP."

Chris couldn't do anything but comply, stopping in his tracks and raising his hands. However, as he did so, the knife was still in his hand.

"I DIDN'T KILL HER, I DIDN'T KILL HER!" Chris shouted.

Unfortunately, the police didn't believe Chris. They thought he was the serial killer.

The police rushed toward Chris, grabbed his arms, and pushed him against the wall, swiftly handcuffing him. Chris continued to protest, repeating, "I DIDN'T DO IT, I DIDN'T DO IT."

But once again, the police didn't believe him.

Police officer Tippit sternly said, "Shut up. You are under arrest for murder."

Officer Tippit proceeded to read Chris his rights: "You have the right to remain silent. Anything you say will be held against you in a court of law. You have the right to an attorney present during questioning. If you cannot afford an attorney, one will be provided for you. If you waive these rights, you may still be questioned by an attorney. Do you understand your rights?" Officer Tippit asked.

"Yes, I do, but I didn't kill this woman," Chris replied.

Despite Chris's plea, the police remained unconvinced. They placed him in the police car and took him to jail. But before doing so, they removed his mask.

Chris Holden Has Been Locked Up for Murder

The police walked over toward the dead woman and noticed that she was half-naked. They began taking pictures of the scene, including the knife with blood splattered all over the alley.

"We got the serial killer," said one of the police officers as he spoke into his radio, relaying the information back to the police station.

"We have the serial killer in custody."

Or so they thought.

There were countless police officers and FBI agents on the scene. Chris was charged with first-degree murder. He repeatedly tried to tell them that he didn't do it, but they refused to believe him.

The FBI agents told Chris that he would need a good lawyer. They showed him pictures of all the murdered women, claiming that he was responsible for their deaths.

Chris insisted that he didn't kill those women. He was only trying to help the woman in the alley. The real killer had gotten away, he explained.

Despite his protests, they still didn't believe him. They booked Chris for murder. He found himself in trouble for a crime he didn't commit.

"Can I call my wife?" Chris asked the police.

"Yes, you can," they replied.

Chris used the telephone in the holding cell to call his wife, June, and explained what had happened. She couldn't believe it.

"I'm coming down there," June said.

June arrived at the police station to talk to Chris. He recounted the events once again, expressing his need for help.

"Honey, you need a lawyer," June told him. "I'll check our bank account to see how much money we have. We need to get you a good lawyer. I'll also find out the amount of your bond so you can come home before your trial."

"I'll be right back," she assured him.

June approached the police chief and inquired about the amount of Chris's bond to secure his release from jail.

The police chief informed her that his bond was set at a million dollars and that he would have to stand trial for all the women he was accused of murdering.

"Yes, he's going to need a really good lawyer to get him out of this, Mrs. Holden," the police chief remarked.

"But my husband didn't kill all of these women," June insisted. "My husband is a good man."

"They saw your husband in the alley with a knife in his hand, on top of this woman he killed. Getting him out of jail is going to be a difficult thing to do, Mrs. Holden," said the police chief. "We have evidence against him. It's going to cost you a million dollars just to get him out on bond, Mrs. Holden. But he still has to go to court."

Mrs. June Holden went to her bank to see how much they had. They only had $35,000 in the bank, which was far from enough to get Chris out of jail. June knew her husband was innocent, but she had to prove it.

She returned to the police station and informed Chris about the million-dollar bond and the money in the bank. "Honey, I'm going to have to find you a lawyer," she said.

Chris replied, "Okay, honey, you do that, and please hurry."

Killer Steve Jones was happy that Chris got caught. He decided to stop his killing spree until Chris was convicted, using the time to cover up his tracks.

Mrs. Holden kissed Chris and went home.

This Is When the Young Perry Mason Begins His First Big Case

June began looking into the yellow pages for a lawyer and saw Perry Mason's name and phone number. She called the next day. At 9:30 a.m., Della answered the telephone.

June said, "Hello, is this Mr. Perry Mason's office?"

Della replied, "Yes, it is, but it is his son's office now. Mr. Perry Mason is no longer with us. You can talk to his son, Burt Mason. He is the new lawyer now."

June asked, "Can I make an appointment to see Mr. Mason?"

Della responded, "Yes, you can. What is your problem?"

June explained, "My husband has been accused of a murder he didn't commit."

Della said, "Okay, Mrs. Holden, Burt will call you."

When June received the call for her appointment, she went to Perry Mason's office.

"Good morning, Mrs. Holden. My name is Mr. Burt Mason," greeted Burt. "I am the son of Perry Mason. My father is deceased. So what can I do for you, Mrs. Holden?"

"My husband's name is Chris, and he is locked up for a murder he did not commit," explained June. "Please, Mr. Mason, please help my husband. I only have $35,000.00 to pay you."

"Okay, Mrs. Holden," responded Burt. "Which jail is your husband locked up in, Mrs. Holden?"

"He is at the city jail downtown," replied Mrs. Holden.

"I will go down to the city jail to talk to him," said Burt.

Della and Mr. Paul Drake were in the office with Burt as he spoke with Mrs. June Holden.

Burt Visits Chris, Who Is in Jail

So Burt went to the city jail to talk to Chris.

The police officer let Burt into the jail cell so he could talk to Chris.

"Hi, my name is Mr. Burt Mason, and I just talked to your wife, Mrs. Holden," greeted Burt. "I am a lawyer, and I am going to try to help you. Now, please tell me what happened."

Chris began recounting the events. "It was on a cold November night at 9:30 p.m. on a Saturday. I was on my way to the grocery store when I heard this woman screaming from an alley on Third and Main Street. I ran, and when I looked down the alley, I saw this woman being stabbed by a person. I ran down the alley trying to help her, and as I approached, the man turned his head, pulled his pants up, and started running away. By the time I reached her, she was already dead. The killer was wearing a mask similar to mine. I picked up the knife, and that's when the police arrested me. They charged me with murder, but I tried to tell them the truth. They didn't believe me. They think I am the serial killer."

"Mr. Mason, I didn't kill that woman or anybody. Please help me," pleaded Chris.

"Okay, Mr. Holden, I will do what I can for you," reassured Burt. "During the trial, I want you to remain silent. Let me do the talking. Once we gather all the evidence on this killer, we will have something to fight within court."

"Okay, Mr. Mason," agreed Chris. "Oh, yes, I also saw a pair of bloody blue rubber gloves on the ground beside her."

"Alright, Mr. Holden," acknowledged Burt. "And one more thing, when you picked up the knife, your fingerprints got on it. That's what the police saw when they found you with the knife in your hand. They also noticed you wearing the same mask as the killer, which made you a suspect and raised suspicions against you."

"And to get started, please tell me what this man looked like," Mr. Holden said Burt.

"He was about six feet tall, and he looked like he was about 154 pounds with small-looking hands," Chris replied.

"Small-looking hands?" asked Burt.

"Yeah, sir," answered Chris.

"Let me see your hands," requested Burt.

Chris showed Burt his hands, and Burt noticed that Chris's hands were big.

"Okay, Mr. Holden," said Burt. "I am going to go now, but I will keep in touch with you and your wife."

"Is there any way I can be at home with my wife until the trial?" asked Chris.

"Unless you have a million-dollar bail bond to get yourself out, no. They are going to keep you in jail until the trial, Mr. Holden," explained Burt. "I'll see you again soon. Be patient, Mr. Holden. This crime is going to take time. You are going to go through a lot of courtroom trials. The other lawyer is going to try to get the jury to find you guilty. But we are going to fight this so you can go home. However, if the jury finds you guilty of this and all the other murders, they are going to give you the death penalty. So again, in the courtroom, you must not do or say anything. Just let me do the talking, Mr. Holden. I'll see you in court."

Burt walked out of the jail cell and proceeded downstairs to the evidence room of the jail. He asked the police officer working there for the knife and the bloody gloves, and requested permission to take a picture of them. Burt wanted to capture images of both sides of the knife and examine any serial numbers present. By tracing the knife's ownership through the serial numbers, he hoped to find the identity of the killer.

When Paul Starts Doing Some Investigation

Burt noticed that the bloody gloves were small and too little to fit on Chris's hands. When Burt examined the numbers on the knife, he saw that the serial number was "NO, TX 9347974," indicating it was a deer hunter knife. Burt took note of this information and called Paul Drake.

At 5:45 p.m. on a Monday evening, Paul answered the phone and said, "Hello, Burt, what's up?"

Burt replied, "Paul, I need you to do something for me. I want you to write down this serial number from the murder knife that I took a picture of and check it out for me."

"Sure thing, Burt. What are the numbers on the knife?" asked Paul.

Burt provided the information, saying, "The numbers are 'NO, TX 9347974.' It's a deer hunter knife."

"Got it, Burt. I'll have to visit a lot of stores to find this number," remarked Paul.

"Have fun," joked Burt.

"Yeah, right," replied Paul. "Oh, and check out and buy some blue gloves, a box of large gloves, and a box of small gloves to take to court."

"Okay, Burt," agreed Paul.

Burt studied a picture of the murder scene and the victim, noting the location of the incident. He also spoke with the coroner, who took pictures of the murdered woman and the stab wounds on her body. Looking at the images made Burt almost sick.

Additionally, Burt obtained the time of the murder. Returning to the cell where Chris was held, he brought two boxes of blue gloves.

"Mr. Holden, here are two types of gloves: the small ones and the large ones," said Burt. "Try on the large gloves."

Chris put on the large gloves, and they fit him. Burt then instructed, "Now try on the small gloves."

Chris attempted to put on the small gloves, but they did not fit his hands.

Examining the picture of the small gloves, Burt placed the actual gloves on the image and found a match.

"Mr. Holden, I had my private investigator, Mr. Paul Drake, find out who bought the knife with the serial numbers on it," Burt explained. "Once he uncovers the purchaser, we will have our killer."

Chris leaned back in his chair and smiled.

The murdered woman's name was Mrs. Sandra Sheffer. She had a husband and three children, whom Steve Jones, the real killer, intended to target next. The thought saddened Chris.

"Yeah, I do too," Burt agreed. "Steve Jones has it on his mind that he's going to kill again. But before he resumes his killing spree, he wants to see if they lock up Chris for the rest of his life or execute him. And if the jury finds Chris guilty, he plans to kill again."

The Dumb Thing Steve Jones Is About to Do

Steve didn't realize that the murder investigation was underway, focusing on the serial numbers of the deer hunting knife and the small gloves, which matched Chris's hands.

Perry Mason, known for his intelligence and success in murder cases, had passed down his skills to his son, Burt, who was on his way to becoming one of the best lawyers.

As the days went by, Chris and Burt appeared in court multiple times. The opposing lawyers did their best to convince the jury of Chris's guilt for first-degree murder. However, Burt managed to persuade Judge Dick Taylor and the jury to give him more time.

Judge Dick Taylor informed Burt that he would grant him just one more day.

Day by day, Paul visited different stores in search of the origin of the deer hunting knife, but he had no luck. Until one day, he arrived at a Walmart store, hoping to find the evidence needed to help Chris.

When Paul Finds the Evidence

Paul entered the Walmart store and made his way to the sporting department, where he asked to speak to the manager. Paul showed the manager the picture of the hunting knife with the serial numbers.

The manager inquired about Paul's identity, to which Paul responded, "My name is Mr. Paul Drake, and I am a private investigator. I am investigating a murder and need some information about this hunting knife." Paul showed the manager the picture of the knife and its corresponding serial numbers, along with the gloves.

Paul asked if the store kept old records or credit card receipts for purchases of such knives. The manager confirmed that they did, and offered to show them to Paul. They proceeded to the manager's office, where he retrieved a book containing the knife and glove records. The numbers on the knife matched the ones in the book.

The store manager also had a photograph of the person who had used a credit card for the purchase, and it showed Steve Jones. Paul exclaimed, "I've got you!" He took a copy of Steve Jones's photo and thanked the manager for the assistance.

Paul left the store and headed towards Burt's home. He showed Burt the picture and Burt smiled, saying, "Thanks." Burt had discovered that Steve Jones was the real criminal, the serial killer, and not Chris.

Burt had also learned that Steve Jones had a criminal record, having been imprisoned multiple times for offenses involving deadly weapons such as guns and knives. He had spent ten years in San

Quentin Prison, and the numbers on the knife he used in this murder matched those from a previous incident where he nearly killed a woman and a man in an alley.

The Setup

Paul asked Burt, "Now that you have all the evidence, what are you going to do?"

"Are you going to call the police and the FBI to apprehend him, Burt?" inquired Paul.

"No, Paul, I have an idea," replied Burt. "And it's a long shot, but it just might work."

"What do you mean, Burt?" Paul asked, curious.

"Some criminals stop their killing spree until the innocent person is convicted. They want to see the outcome in court and take pleasure when an innocent person is found guilty," explained Burt. "So, here's my plan: we'll set a trap."

Paul questioned, "What exactly do you have in mind, Burt?"

Burt laid out the details of his plan. "During the court proceedings, keep an eye out for Steve Jones. If you spot him entering the courtroom, don't say a word. Instead, inform the police and ask them to lock the doors. If they inquire why, just tell them it's because we are searching for a criminal entering the courtroom."

"Okay, Burt, I'll do that," agreed Paul.

Burt then went to the city jail to inform Chris about Steve Jones and the plan for the courtroom. He instructed Chris to remain silent and do nothing.

Meanwhile, Steve Jones was living in seclusion, hiding out in an old house deep in the woods, watching television. Unbeknownst to him, the news broke about the capture of the serial killer. During an interview, when asked about the killer's identity, Jeff, the lawyer, falsely named Chris Holden. Jeff confidently predicted that Chris would be convicted for all the crimes.

The public strongly believed that Chris was the serial killer and wanted to see him spend the rest of his life in jail, or worse. The upcoming courtroom trial would be televised live, and Steve Jones decided he would be present. Little did he know that he had been discovered and that a trap was about to be sprung.

The Preliminary Hearing Courtroom Drama and the Witness

December 21, 1993, at 9:30 a.m., the murder trial began. This trial would determine Mr. Holden's innocence or guilt. As the trial commenced, Jeff urged the jury to find Chris Holden guilty of murder. Judge Dick Taylor then asked Jeff if he had any witnesses to substantiate the accused's guilt.

Jeff confidently replied that he did indeed have witnesses. He claimed to have personally conducted the murder investigation and presented five to six witnesses in court who had allegedly seen Chris commit the murder of Mrs. Sandra Sheffer on November 9.

As the trial proceedings unfolded, Chris was escorted into the courtroom wearing a gray outfit with *City Jail* written on the back. He was also handcuffed and had leg restraints. People filed into the courtroom, and among them was Steve Jones, who entered quietly. Paul noticed Steve's presence and approached a police officer, instructing him to lock the courtroom doors. The officer promptly followed Paul's orders. Paul was taken aback, not expecting Burt's plan to work so effectively.

With everyone settled, the trial officially began. The police officer in the courtroom announced, "All rise for Judge Dick Taylor." As Judge Dick Taylor emerged from the courtroom's back room, everyone stood up in respect.

When the Jury Was About to Come to Their Decision

"Please be seated," instructed the police officer.

As the judge took his seat, the people in the courtroom followed suit and sat down as well. Burt Mason, Della Street, and Paul Drake were present, along with the killer, Steve Jones. Steve sat in the back row, thinking that he would go unnoticed. However, Burt, Paul, and Della were keenly aware of his presence.

Lawyer Jeff Jason began presenting his case. He addressed the jury, saying, "Ladies and gentlemen of the jury, we are here to discuss the serial killer, the defendant Mr. Chris Holden. This man has allegedly murdered over twenty-five, possibly thirty women. When he committed his latest murder on the night of November, the police arrested him, and he has been charged with this crime of murder. I ask you, ladies and gentlemen of the jury, to find Mr. Holden guilty for all of these murders as he took the lives of these women in cold blood. I plead for a guilty verdict and seek the death penalty. Thank you," concluded Jeff.

The Witness

Jeff then turned to address the judge. "Your Honor, I want to question some witnesses who claim to have seen the defendant kill Ms. Sheffer on the night of November."

"Okay," said Judge Taylor. "I have been conducting my own investigation into this murder, and I have six witnesses here in court whom I would like to put on the witness stand for questioning," said Jeff.

The judge responded, "Bring on your witnesses, Mr. Jason."

"For my first witness, I would like to call Mr. Paul Lindbergh to the stand," said Jeff.

Judge Taylor instructed, "Will Mr. Paul Lindbergh please take the stand?"

Paul Lindbergh took his place on the stand.

"Mr. Lindbergh, what is your occupation?" asked Jeff.

"I am a janitor who works at the food market," replied Mr. Lindbergh.

Jeff continued, "Do you work near the alley where Mrs. Shanda Sheffer was murdered, Mr. Lindbergh? Did you work that night on the ninth of November around 9:30 p.m.?"

"Yes, I was working that night," confirmed Mr. Lindbergh.

Jeff inquired further, "Did you hear someone screaming in the alley that night, Mr. Lindbergh?"

Mr. Lindbergh responded, "When I was cleaning up the store, I heard screaming in the alley."

Jeff pressed on "So, what did you do, Mr. Lindbergh?"

Mr. Lindbergh explained, "I ran to the side door that faced the alley, and I opened it. When I looked, I saw this man on top of a woman, stabbing her."

"Is this man whom you saw here in this courtroom, Mr. Lindbergh?" asked Jeff.

"Yes," said Mr. Lindbergh, pointing at Chris.

"Thank you, Mr. Lindbergh," said Jeff.

Judge Taylor then asked Burt if he had any questions for Mr. Lindbergh. Burt replied, "No, Your Honor."

"Okay, Mr. Lindbergh, you may return to your seat," stated the judge.

Mr. Lindbergh returned to his seat.

"I would like to call Mrs. Jean Hanley to the stand, please," said Jeff.

"Please take the witness stand, Mrs. Hanley," instructed the judge.

Mrs. Jean Hanley took her place on the witness stand. Jeff began his questioning, asking Mrs. Hanley about her occupation.

"I am a salesperson who sells clothes to people," answered Mrs. Hanley.

"Okay, Mrs. Hanley, on the night of November, did you hear screaming in the alley near Third Street?" asked Jeff.

"Yes," replied Mrs. Hanley.

Jeff continued, "On that November night, what were you doing when you heard the screaming, Mrs. Hanley, and what did you do?"

Mrs. Hanley explained, "I was walking home from work, and I happened to be walking down Third Street and Main Street when I heard screaming coming from an alley. I ran to see where it was coming from, and when I looked down the alley, I saw a man stabbing a woman. I ran into a nearby food store to seek help and called the police."

Jeff then asked, "Mrs. Hanley, do you see the man who was stabbing the woman?"

Mrs. Hanley pointed her finger at Chris.

"Thank you, Mrs. Hanley," said Jeff.

The judge then asked Burt if he had any questions for Mrs. Hanley, to which Burt replied, “No, Your Honor.”

The judge concluded, “You may return to your seat, Mrs. Hanley. Mr. Jason, you may call your next witness.”

“I would like to call Mr. Bill Ferry to the stand,” said Jeff.

“Mr. Ferry, please come to the witness stand,” instructed Judge Taylor.

Mr. Ferry took his place on the witness stand.

Jeff began by asking, “Mr. Ferry, what is your occupation?”

Mr. Ferry responded, “I am a teacher at Los Angeles University. I teach English.”

Jeff continued, “Okay, Mr. Ferry, where were you when Mrs. Sandra Sheffer was being stabbed to death?”

Mr. Ferry explained, “I was in the store doing some shopping, and when I came out and was about to get into my car, I heard yelling and screaming. I ran to the alley and saw a man with a black mask stabbing a woman. I yelled at him to stop, but he continued stabbing her. Before I could reach the alley to help her, another man wearing the same black mask was running down the alley.”

Jeff questioned further, “You said you saw another man running down the alley with the same kind of mask on. What did he do?”

Mr. Ferry replied, “The man with the mask on was running away, and he ran out of the alley. All I saw was the man who was on top of her, stabbing the woman to death.”

Burt realized that Chris was not the man who killed Mrs. Sandra Sheffer when he saw this other man running from the crime scene, but he did not speak up just yet.

“I could not see the man who was running away because of the mask he was wearing on his face,” said Mr. Ferry.

Jeff continued, “Okay, Mr. Ferry, the man you did see on top of the woman, do you see him here in this courtroom?”

Mr. Ferry confirmed, “Yes, I do.” He pointed his finger at Chris and stated, “I do believe it was that man over there who was doing the stabbing.”

Jeff requested, “Please, Mr. Ferry, point your finger at him.”

Mr. Ferry pointed at Chris, and Jeff thanked him, saying, "Okay, Mr. Ferry, thank you. You may be seated."

Jeff then asked Burt if he had any questions for Mr. Ferry.

Burt replied, "No, Your Honor."

Jeff proceeded to call Mr. John Clayton to the witness stand. "Mr. Clayton, please take the witness stand," said Jeff. After Mr. Clayton took the stand, Jeff inquired about his occupation.

Mr. Clayton responded, "I work for the Los Angeles gas company."

Jeff continued his questioning, "On the night of the murder, where were you?"

Mr. Clayton explained, "Me and a friend of mine were just getting off from work, and we were on our way home. We stopped at a store on Third Street and Main to buy beer and some ice for the beer. Around 9:30 p.m., while we were at the store, me and my friend heard yelling and screaming. I asked my friend if he heard something like somebody yelling and screaming, and he said yes. So we got out of the truck and ran down the street. We looked down the alley and saw a man with a mask on stabbing this woman. My friend and I started yelling down the alley, telling this person to stop what he was doing to that woman."

Jeff questioned further, "Who is your friend? What is his name?"

Mr. Clayton replied, "His name is Bob Terry."

Jeff inquired, "How come you and Mr. Terry didn't go down the alley and try to stop this killer?"

Mr. Clayton explained, "I guess we were afraid to get involved and get too close to this maniac, so we ran to the truck. I got on my radio and called for the police."

Jeff then asked Mr. Clayton, "Do you see this maniac here in this court?"

Mr. Clayton identified Chris and said, "Yes, I do. It was that man sitting over there."

Jeff requested Mr. Clayton to point at him, and Mr. Clayton pointed at Chris. Jeff concluded, "Okay, Mr. Clayton, you can return to your seat."

The judge then asked Burt if he had any questions for Mr. Clayton. Burt replied, "No, Your Honor."

Jeff proceeded, "I would like to call Mr. Busch Chouteau to the witness stand."

"Mr. Chouteau, please take the witness stand," said the judge.

It was 10:00 a.m., and the time was running out for Chris. Burt knew he had to get Paul Drake up on the witness stand before the break and before the real killer, Steve Jones, could get away.

Jeff asked Mr. Chouteau, "What is your occupation?"

Mr. Chouteau replied, "I am a street cleaner who works for the city of Los Angeles. I clean streets with a street sweeper."

"On the night of the murder in November, tell me where you were and how you witnessed the murder, Mr. Chouteau."

Mr. Chouteau explained, "I had just finished work, and as I was walking down the street, I was about to go to a bus stop on Third Street. That's when I heard someone screaming and yelling from an alley. I ran to the alley with a few other people, and when I looked down, I saw a man with a mask on stabbing this beautiful woman to death. I wanted to help, but I was in shock and couldn't do anything. So I ran into a nearby food store, yelling for someone to call the police and report a woman being murdered."

Jeff then asked, "Okay, Mr. Chouteau, do you see the killer here in this court?"

Mr. Chouteau identified Chris and said, "Yes, I do. It's that man over there." He pointed his finger at Chris. Jeff thanked him and allowed Mr. Chouteau to return to his seat.

Burt was asked if he had any questions for Mr. Chouteau, to which he replied, "No, Your Honor."

Jeff believed he had Burt where he wanted him and thought he would convict Chris for the murders. There was only one more witness left to testify about the murder, and that was Police Officer J. T. Tippit. Jeff requested Officer Tippit to come to the witness stand. Officer Tippit walked up and sat down.

Jeff began by asking, "Officer Tippit, how long have you been on the police force?"

Officer Tippit responded, "I have been on the police force for ten years, sir."

"And in your line of duty, you have seen a lot of homicides, isn't that right?"

Officer Tippit confirmed, "Yes, sir."

Jeff then asked, "Okay, where were you on the night of November when Mrs. Sandra Sheffer was being murdered? Were you on duty that night?"

"When my partner and I were on duty that night, we received a call from my dispatcher informing us of a stabbing in an alley on Third and Main Street. When we arrived, I saw a man on top of a woman with a deer hunter's knife in his hand," Officer Tippit explained.

Jeff asked, "Was he stabbing the woman?"

Officer Tippit replied, "No, he was not stabbing her at the time we arrived and saw him."

Jeff inquired, "So what did you do next?"

Officer Tippit responded, "I arrested him for the murder."

Jeff questioned, "Are you sure that the man in this courtroom was the one committing the killing?"

Officer Tippit stated, "I believe so, sir, because he had a mask on and was holding the knife."

Jeff further asked, "Is the killer present in this courtroom?"

Officer Tippit pointed his finger at Chris and said, "Yes, sir."

Officer Tippit was the final witness in the murder case, and the jury looked at Chris, convinced of his guilt.

Just as Jeff was about to present his closing argument to the jury based on the testimonies he had obtained, Burt stood up and objected, saying, "I object, Your Honor. Just because the police saw Mr. Holden at the scene of the crime doesn't mean he did it. My client was merely trying to help the woman when he was arrested. Wearing a mask that resembles the serial killer's mask does not make him a killer. Many people wear masks when it's very cold outside."

Jeff objected, saying, "I can understand that, but the defendant had the murder weapon, a bloody deer hunter's knife, in his hand. If the defendant was trying to help the woman, then why would he have the knife in his hand and be seen with it when the police arrived at the scene?"

Burt countered, saying, "That still doesn't mean he is the killer. Did Officer Tippit see my client stabbing the woman at the time of the arrest?" Burt answered his own question, "No, he didn't."

Jeff interjected, "Yes, it does."

When Burt Tells His Last Testimony

Jeff stated, "There you have it, ladies and gentlemen of the jury. The defendant Chris Holden killed Mrs. Sandra Sheffer and numerous other women in cold blood. He is the serial killer and should be punished for his crimes."

Burt objected, saying, "I object, Your Honor. I would like to bring forth one witness. But before I do, I would like to address all the witnesses that Mr. Jeff has presented. You claim that my client is the serial killer based on seeing him with a mask and a knife in his hand, accusing him of stabbing this woman in the alley on that Saturday night in November."

Burt continued, "Half of you are uncertain whether he is the killer, and half of you have doubts about him being the serial killer. My client told me he was trying to help the woman and happened to be wearing a mask due to the cold night. Just because he picked up the knife does not mean he was stabbing her. Why would some of you sit there and lie, saying he was stabbing the woman when you know he didn't do it? Some of you want to see someone convicted of a crime you never witnessed. All you saw was a man wearing a mask and holding a knife."

Burt concluded, "Now, you have heard this story and received the sensationalized version of this man committing the crime. But before you convict him, I would like to call a witness to the stand who will tell you the truth."

When Paul Drake Takes the Stand

"Your Honor, I would like to call Mr. Paul Drake to the witness stand, if I may," Burt requested. The judge granted permission, and Burt proceeded, "I would like to call Mr. Paul Drake to the witness stand."

Paul walked up to the witness stand and took his seat.

Burt began questioning him, "Mr. Paul Drake, what is your occupation?"

Paul replied, "I am a private investigator."

"Who are you working for, Mr. Drake?"

Paul answered, "I am working for you, Mr. Mason."

Burt then asked, "Okay, so tell me, Mr. Drake, what did I ask you to do?"

"You gave me a picture of a hunting knife with some serial numbers on it."

Burt further inquired, "What did I ask you to do with the picture of the serial numbers from the knife, Paul?"

Paul answered, "You asked me to try to find the store where the knife came from."

Burt asked, "What did you come up with, Paul?"

Paul replied, "I found out that the knife belongs to a man named Steve Jones. Here is his picture from a credit card at a Walmart store."

Steve's eyes widened as he looked around at everyone in the courtroom.

When Steve Jones Gets Caught

Burt asked, "Now, is this killer here in this courtroom today?"

Paul responded, "Yes, he is."

Paul proceeded to show the judge and jury the picture of the knife, along with a picture of Steve Jones and other evidence related to the murder case. As Paul displayed the picture of Steve Jones, everyone in the courtroom turned to look at him.

Suddenly Steve Jones jumped up and pulled out a knife from his pocket. He grabbed a woman and held the knife against her neck, warning everyone to stay back or he would harm her. "Open the door!" Steve demanded, urging the police officer to comply.

Meanwhile, numerous police officers surrounded the courthouse, and a SWAT team positioned themselves on the rooftop, armed and ready to respond when Steve exited the building.

Burt, Paul, and Della Street chose to remain inside the courtroom to ensure their safety and avoid any harm.

When Steve Tries to Escape and Gets Captured

When Steve emerged outside the courthouse and saw the multitude of police officers, he shouted, "GET BACK OR I WILL KILL HER!"

A woman from the SWAT team, positioned on top of a nearby building with her rifle, spotted Steve and took aim. She fired a shot, hitting Steve in the shoulder. The impact caused him to drop the knife and fall to the ground. The police quickly apprehended him, handcuffed his arms, and placed him in a police car. Steve was then transported to the hospital for treatment of his gunshot wound.

Following his release from the hospital, Steve Jones was taken to jail, where he received a life sentence. Meanwhile, Chris Holden, now proven innocent, was able to return home to his family. Burt received payment for his services, and in recognition of their efforts in capturing the serial killer Steve Jones, Burt, Della, and Paul were honored with an award by the mayor.

Back at Mason's Office

Burt, Paul, and Della Street were gathered in the office, discussing the serial killing case.

Paul expressed his curiosity, "Burt, I still can't figure it out. How did you know Steve Jones was going to come to the courtroom? How did you know?"

Burt replied, "I didn't know, Paul. When Steve Jones showed up in the courtroom, it was a surprise to me as well. But even if he hadn't shown up, he would have been caught eventually because of the serial number on the knife, the ill-fitting gloves, and all the other evidence pointing to Mr. Jones. You see, Paul, Mr. Holden didn't commit any of those murders. It was just a matter of time."

Paul remarked, "Like father, like son."

Burt thanked Paul for his comment and the support he had provided throughout the case.

After Burt's victory in the serial killing case, Burt, Paul, Della, and Isabella celebrated at Burt's home. Mr. and Mrs. Holden, grateful for Burt's help in proving Chris's innocence, joined in the celebration. Later, they all visited Perry Mason's grave to pay their respects. Isabella placed flowers on the grave while Burt looked at the plaque displaying Perry's birth and death dates.

Burt spoke to the grave, saying, "Thank you, Dad. Thank you for everything."

They all held hands and said a prayer in memory of Perry. Burt felt a mixture of sadness for Perry's passing but also gratitude for the knowledge and skills Perry had imparted to him. "I love you, Dad, and I always will."

A Job Well Done

Isabella hugged and kissed Burt on his jaw, expressing her affection. Perry Mason was a remarkable man in his time, and as they left the cemetery, Burt, Paul, and Della would always remember the man they knew as Perry Mason, both the seasoned lawyer and the young Perry Mason.

Burt, Paul, and Della took on a wide range of cases, including murders, divorces, child support, garnishments, and more. Burt even helped secure the release of individuals from jail in drug-related cases, assisted the homeless, and made donations whenever possible. Through their impactful work, they became legendary figures, known as some of the greatest lawyers who ever lived.

The end

The Treasure of a Child's Heart

BY BURNETT LEE DORRIS (MAY 1986)

January 17, 2001

The treasure of a child's heart is when God blesses a man and woman with a beautiful child from the start. From the moment he or she arrives, it brings happiness into our lives. And with the treasure of a child's heart, our love will never falter. We will always love them and never hide from them, cherishing them as our little buttercup. We will always be glad to know we are happy and not sad.

With the treasure of a child's heart, they will always bring us happiness and joy, smiling as they play with their little toys. They will keep us laughing and ask about the love we share that is real. Knowing that someone is there to provide love and care, our love will never fall apart with the treasure of a child's heart.

In my book I wrote
Titanic and the Second Voyage
The Race Is On
and my writing continues.

THE TRAGEDY AT SUGAR CREEK

A brief story

BURNETT LEE DORRIS

My name is Mr. John Carter. I have been driving school buses for the past twenty-seven years, and the story I am about to tell you is an incredible and unbelievable one. I am a school bus driver for Student Transit, and like all the other drivers, I come to work and do my route every day.

Sometimes we also get charter assignments. As a school bus driver, I love doing charters. It keeps me busy during the day, allows me to make more money, and I enjoy being out on the streets, roads, and highways regardless of the weather. I actually prefer doing charters over regular routes.

On April 6, 2018, a Friday, I was sitting in the break room around 10:00 or 10:30 a.m. I had an early pickup for my students, so the dispatcher, Lisa Goldman, approached me and asked if I would like to do a quick charter. Initially, I was inclined to decline because I had just finished a charter, and it was almost time for me to start my route. However, I quickly changed my mind and agreed to do it. Lisa gave me a charter to go out to Sugar Creek, pick up some people, and drop them off at their destination.

Little did I know that this charter would take me on some narrow roads that resembled driving along the side of a valley or mountain. The roads felt narrow, with deep and potentially dangerous cliffs. From the heights, I could see people's homes below, and it was evident that driving recklessly or losing control of the vehicle could be fatal, regardless of the type of vehicle or one's driving skills.

I was driving a sixty-five-passenger school bus. Lisa provided me with the charter sheet and directions to reach Sugar Creek. I entered my bus and began the journey. The directions indicated that I should take 44 west, then I-270 south, and exit at exit 3 onto Gravis. From there, I was to make a right turn and continue until I reached Sugar Creek.

Upon examining the street map Lisa gave me, initially, I only saw the instruction to turn right on Sugar Creek. I didn't notice the direction to make a left turn until the last minute when I saw another bus making the left turn. It was either the other driver or Ms. Lisa who informed me about the left turn. I had to turn my bus around and drive down that road in an attempt to catch up to the other bus.

As I ventured down that road, deep inside, I felt a strong sense of fear due to its treacherous nature. I was becoming increasingly nervous while driving a big, long school bus up and down that road with perilous cliffs nearby. My heart raced as I continued navigating the mountains and curves, desperately searching for the school bus.

With each passing moment, the road seemed to grow more hazardous. I muttered to myself, "Where is this school bus?" The other driver, also operating a sixty-five-passenger school bus, seemed to have vanished. I couldn't find her anywhere. Dispatcher Lisa contacted me, wondering about my whereabouts. I explained that I was searching for Old Sugar Creek Road, but I had mistakenly ended up on Old Sugar Creek Road. It was at a stop along the way that I noticed another street with the same name, compounding my confusion.

I found myself lost, driving back and forth along the same road after realizing my error. I navigated the highs and lows of the winding curves, desperately searching for the school bus. Despite the dispatcher's attempts to provide me with directions, I struggled to find my way. Lisa could see my location on her website and informed me that I had gone too far and needed to turn around.

Thinking she was trying to direct me to the location of the other bus, I turned my bus around and began driving back the same way I came. As I reached the top of the hill, I had to come to a stop at a stop sign. While descending the hill and riding on my brakes, they began to emit smoke. Suddenly my brakes stopped working, leaving me hurtling down the curving side hill road at an alarming speed.

Too frightened to contact the dispatcher, I struggled to maintain control of the school bus. However, I ultimately lost control while attempting to negotiate a curve, causing the bus to veer off the high cliff. Tumbling down the side of the road, I crashed into twelve homes, five parked cars, and three motorcycles. Amidst the chaos, I suffered a massive heart attack and succumbed to death.

When I returned to the base with the school bus, I informed Ms. Lisa about the incident. Ms. Lisa questioned me, saying, "If you had a massive heart attack and died while the school bus was causing all this damage to homes, cars, and motorcycles, how come you are still alive and the bus doesn't have a scratch on it?"

In response, I chuckled and said to Ms. Lisa, "I died, and this is my afterlife. None of this ever happened. Ha, ha, ha!"

The end

EVERYBODY GETS HOME SAFE

BURNETT LEE DORRIS

In a school bus, everybody gets home safe.

Since when?
The Rock and roll l. p.
By Burnett Lee Dorris
When did the first
rock and roll l p,
come out?
When people started getting
hit upside their heads with
hem, and they call it rocking
and rolling.
You keep your school bus clean and
fuel 5-16-18
By Burnett Lee Dorris
Dispatcher: Mr. Dorris, I see that you
keep your school bus clean and fuel.
Dorris: Yes, I keep my school bus clean
and pregnant.
Why do women funs with dogs?
By Burnett Lee Dorris 5-16-18
Honey: Say, dear, why do women be running?
down the street with dogs
Dear: Because they run out of Tampaxes.

The Stars of the Hall of Fame

I've seen many famous actors and singers who have become stars and achieved great success. They were in the right place at the right time, working tirelessly to earn their star on the Hollywood Walk of Fame. Their names are engraved in gold in the Hall of Fame, but let me tell you, reaching for that star life is no easy task.

You must possess some extraordinary talent to attain the pot of gold at the end of the rainbow. Being rich and famous, riding in a luxurious limousine, living a lavish life, and traveling the world in a private jet or airplane are all part of the dream. Seeing your name in lights as people smile and take pictures of you on the red carpet, while you graciously sign autographs, is an incredible feeling.

Walking the streets of Hollywood, all the stars on the Walk of Fame light up, and I can't help but feel uplifted by their presence, even when I stroll through the smaller version of Hollywood in University City here in St. Louis.

Successful individuals from St. Louis have achieved great things and become superstars. However, as time passes, stars may pass away, leaving behind cherished memories. Despite the challenges that come with success, I believe pursuing a successful life would be fulfilling. As a writer, I have dreams of achieving success and living a prosperous life. I believe I owe it to myself to strive for riches and fame, to have my name engraved in gold and placed among the stars in the Hall of Fame.

Aretha Franklin

THE QUEEN OF SOUL
1942–2018

There has always been a joyous moment in my life when it comes to soul music that lifts our spirits. We would dance to her music and sing along to her songs. She was the embodiment of soul in our dreams, and I felt immense pride in knowing the queen of soul, Aretha Franklin.

She was a divine connection to God, singing soul and gospel music that resonated with people all over the world. She was our source of inspiration for soulful music. Her loss is not only that of a beautiful woman, but also a loss of immense talent.

As she sang, she brought tremendous joy and happiness into our lives with her incredible voice, much like the godfather of soul, James Brown, who would get down but is no longer with us. We feel a profound sadness at the loss of such talented individuals.

God had sent an angel from heaven with a special kind of talent that we all loved so dearly. This angel could sing, play the piano, and write her own songs. She would grace the stage and astound the world with her abilities. The sun shone so brightly when she was around, but the sky grew cloudy and the rain began to fall.

When the rain ceased, our angel was gone. God came for her and took her back home, this time forever. Alongside leaving her family behind, she left us with her beautiful music that we will cherish forever. We all love her, and we will deeply miss our singing angel.

Rest in peace, our singing angel. And that is you, Aretha Franklin. You will always be the queen of our souls.

The Treasure of a Child's Heart

January 17, 2001

The treasure of a child's heart is when God blesses a man and woman with a beautiful child from the stars. From the moment he or she arrives, it brings happiness into our lives. And with the treasure of a child's heart, our love would never falter. We would always love them and never try to hide from them. We would never give them up and affectionately call them our little buttercups.

With the treasure of a child's heart, they will always bring us happiness, joys, and smiles when they play with their little toys. They will always keep us laughing and ask about how we make them feel loved and cared for. To know that someone is there for them, providing love and care. And with the treasure of a child's heart, our love will never fall apart.

The Lifestyles of the Rich and Famous

(ORIGINAL WRITTEN MAY 27, 1986)

How rich do you wanna be?
How rich do you wanna be?
The lifestyles of the rich and famous
is where the people makes it big in Hollywood
and I wish it could happen for me
to live the life of

(Chorus)

The lifestyles of the rich and famous
The lifestyle of the rich and famous
where fortune is the final frontier
and how that duck get that kind of luck in digging
the scene in riding in a limousine in repeat chorus
The lifestyles of the rich and famous
The lifestyles of the rich and famous
where fortune is the final frontier
in living in a big house on the mountain top and live to be a famous singer
are a movie star that will take you far by being in repeat chorus
The lifestyles of the rich and famous
The lifestyles of the rich and famous

where fortune is the final frontier
and tell me how that duck can get that kind of luck in digging the scene in riding in a limousine where the rich and famous be signing autographs and they would be up for grabs

(In repeat chorus)

The lifestyles of the rich and famous
The lifestyles of the rich and famous
where fortune is the final frontier
where only the in crowd is allowed getting an Academy Award and I would adore more from being in

(Repeat chorus)

The lifestyles of the rich and famous
The lifestyles of the rich and famous
where fortune is the final frontier
and how rich do you wanna be how rich do you wanna be in living

(Repeat chorus)

The lifestyles of the rich and famous
The lifestyles of the rich and famous
where fortune is the final frontier
The lifestyles of the rich and famous where fortune is the final frontier

Other Books by Burnett Lee Dorris -

The Long Orange Rides Again
A comedy western

Titanic and the Second Voyage
The Race is On

The Legend of Joe Darrion and the Chicago Blues
A baseball story

About the Author

A brief biography of Burnett Lee Dorris:

My name is Mr. Burnett Lee Dorris, and I was born and raised in Saint Louis, Missouri, on December 28, 1954.

As a child, I had a deep love for music, especially during the Motown years when artists like Smokey Robinson and the Temptations, along with other Motown families, were making a big impact. However, during that time, before I turned thirty years old, I had no knowledge or experience in writing poems, song lyrics, or short stories.

It was during my time living in Bakersfield, California, from 1978 to 1998, before I moved to Los Angeles, that I began to explore my passion for writing. In 1985, while still in Bakersfield, I engaged in discussions with friends about how singers would write songs based on their personal lives, as well as the power of poetry.

Inspired by these conversations, I made the decision to pursue writing. Today I am deeply passionate about writing and take joy in sharing my creations with the world. I am grateful to God and Jesus for making my dreams come true.

Through my writing, I aim to reach out to readers and share my imagination, inviting them into the realms of fiction and beyond. I appreciate the opportunity to express my unique perspective and connect with others through the written word. Thank you for joining me on this journey.

www.ingramcontent.com/pod-product-compliance
Lightning Source LLC
LaVergne TN
LVHW052036111125
825503LV00012B/749

* 9 7 9 8 8 9 0 6 1 4 8 0 3 *